I0533628

Rolling In Hot!

A Vietnam War

Novelette

By

James Mattison

Rolling In Hot!

A Vietnam War

Novelette

© James Mattison

All rights reserved
All characters are fictional
except as noted.

ISBN: 979-8-9934056-0-5

Rohnert Park, CA

Introduction

Night after night, from dusk to dawn, dedicated USAF airmen gathered aboard their gunships, answering the quiet but urgent summons of war.

Above the jungles and mountains, they became shadows in the sky—silent hunters armed with technology that could pierce the darkest night. Through the green glow of night vision, their adversaries could no longer hide behind the cloak of darkness. Every movement, every flicker of heat, betrayed an enemy's position.

For these men, the mission was never abstract. It had faces—those of the soldiers and civilians on the ground who counted on them for survival. It had a pulse—the steady beat of the engines, the hiss of the radios, the sharp command to engage.

They did not fly for glory, but for each other, for those they protected, and for the unseen threads that bound them to the battlefield below.

Their mission: take the war to the enemy and return home alive.

Their stories live on, handed down through generations –

In 1968, I was an airplane mechanic at an Air Force base. By being in the right place, at the right time, I was selected by the US Air Force to become a Combat Airman.

In record time, I was sent to the Altitude Chamber to start my Aircrew training. Shortly afterwards, I received orders for further training in Ohio.

I was told to dispose of my car and any personal belongings that didn't fit in my duffel bag, as I would never return to my original base. I joined the Air Force to be an airplane mechanic, but now I will be flying as an aircrew member. My life was changing rapidly.

I was trained as an Aerial Gunner on the AC-119G Shadow gunship.

Just after Christmas, my unit and I left for Vietnam.

At first, we flew missions to familiarize ourselves with combat operations. This was an actual war, and we had to learn how to do our jobs while enemy soldiers were shooting at us.

Soon, we were considered 'Combat Ready' and were sent to our assigned air base.

I was part of an eight-man crew: a pilot, a copilot, a flight engineer, two navigators, two gunners, and an illuminator operator.

Fast forward to September 1969.

We were tasked with disrupting an enemy attack that threatened to overrun a US Army Special Forces Camp at Duc Phuong.

Chapter One
The Battle at Duc Phuong

Finally, the monsoon season is over.

We will no longer fly for hours, unable to see the ground. However, our enemy, the NVA or VC, will now be able to hear and see us.

Tonight, we are scheduled to fly on the 2200 mission. At the helm is Colonel Mack, with Major Williams as copilot. Captains Baker and Paulson will be the Navigator and NOS (Night Observation Scope) Operator.

I'm Sgt Matthews, the Bravo Gunner, aka "Matt", paired up with Alpha Gunner SSgt Fontaine, aka "Barry." Rounding out the enlisted crew are Flight Engineer TSgt Roberts and SSgt Jenkins as our Illuminator Operator/Medic.

Before pre-flighting our aircraft, I will catch the crew bus to the flightline cafeteria to pick up lunch for the crew. I'll also get stainless steel 5-gallon jugs of coffee and ice water.

The crew bus stops at the Enlisted quarters to pick up Barry, then takes us to our plane for tonight's mission.

Oh, good, it's 851 tonight, I said to Barry. 851 was a good plane, and the crew chief took such loving care of her that she always brought us home.

Once there, we preflight the gun bay and check the aircraft forms for notes.

Leaving the lunches and 5-gallon jugs on the plane, we depart for the Pre-mission Intel briefing.

Tonight's mission is scheduled "Armed Reconnaissance, or airborne alert."

The Navigators were given coordinates for us to fly to and set up a holding pattern. We'll be on airborne alert for the entire five-hour mission. Intel will inform us of possible enemy action, provide after-action reports from last night's activity, and wrap it all up with Escape and Evasion information.

The entire crew returns to the plane and boards her in preparation for taxi and launch.

As I climb aboard, I notice some of the cargo straps securing the ammunition boxes have come loose. I was cinching up everything when Barry came up on the intercom: "Hey Matt, we're ready for engine start. If you're finished, come up front and strap in."

Barry and I, Jenkins, our Illuminator Operator, and Roberts, our Flight Engineer, took the four troop seats in front of the gun bay.

Before launching, Roberts was up on the flight deck monitoring engine performance for engine start and taxi. Engine start was a raucous operation, involving the rotation of the two giant radial engines. As engine number one coughed and sputtered to life, a massive cloud of white smoke flooded the revetment. Moments later, the monster engine smoothed out, followed by the start of the number two engine, again amid billowing plumes of white smoke.

Mack ran both engines up to high rpms and back down to idle. Satisfied that they performed properly, he called for chocks to be pulled, and the crew chief and his assistants marshalled us out of revetment.

The extreme heat of the Southeast Asian daytime caused unevenness in the taxiway. As we taxied to takeoff position, the plane bounced up and down. It made for quite the ride. The best ride – the takeoff – was to come. Shortly before we arrived at the end of the runway, Roberts came down from the flight deck and strapped in.

Once lined up with the runway centerline, Mack ran the engines up to max take-off power, released the brakes, and away we went!

Mr. Toad's Wild Ride wasn't this scary!

As our plane neared the end of the runway, Mack pulled back on his control wheel, and we slowly left the ground. Shortly after liftoff, the landing gear retracted into the landing gear bay with loud clattering thumps as the bay doors closed and locked.

And so began tonight's mission as Shadow 62.

Our patrol area was the Vietnamese Central Highlands. This area was rife with enemy activity, containing numerous Special Forces Camps and the Ho Chi Minh Trail.

After flying west about 75 miles from our home base, we arrived at our assigned location.

Mack turned the controls over to Williams and came down to the gun bay to take a leak and get some coffee. Filling his Styrofoam cup, he looked towards us in the troop seats with a polite smile as he climbed back up to the flight deck.

Barry was stretched out on top of the ammo cans. I got myself a coffee and returned to my seat.

As I settled into the troop seat, I reflected on last year as a flightline mechanic and this year as an Aerial Gunner, flying perhaps my 100th combat mission.

Barry was a Staff Sergeant, and I was a mere Buck Sergeant. Barry has barely a year more time in service than I, but his leadership experience has imparted wisdom beyond his years. He had already completed a tour of duty as an AC-47 Spooky gunner.

After nine months in combat, I had almost as much experience as Barry. Although I had never flown with him, we were experienced enough to function well together.

The loud crackle of the intercom broke my dream state. Listening intently, I glanced over at Barry, who had just sat up.

I nodded in response to his direction to prepare for the pre-target checklist. As gunners, we developed simple hand signals to communicate, so as not to interfere with intercom and radio traffic. We each carried a checklist in our flight suit calf pocket. He held up his checklist and made a gun-like hand signal, pointing at it. This was our predetermined signal for "Pretarget." We prepared our guns for firing, by removing the safing sectors and installing the ammunition feed units. We kept the arming switches in the SAFE position.

Our Aircraft Commander directed the arming of our guns.

The crackle of the intercom cleared up for the Airborne Command Centers directive, "Your target is a Special Forces camp that's receiving incoming mortars at this time, and they expect a ground attack later. Yankee

Uniform 4304, contact Nifty Tanks on Fox Mike 48 decimal 80, how copy?

Copy all, 62 (call signs were often shortened for convenience).

Command Center - Roger, your target is now classified as a TIC (Troops In Contact).

Troops In Contact is the situation where Allied troops are engaging with the enemy, and in need of (CAS), Close Air Support.

We were directed to support the Special Forces Camp at Duc Phuong, about 12 miles from the Cambodian border.

We were 80 miles out – 20 minutes at full throttle.

Ground controller "Mustang" came up on the radio: Babe, uh, can you see the flares and all the activity?
62 -- We'll do everything we can for you. We're still quite a ways from the area, though.

Mustang - You're gonna probably be tied up with a little bad weather, but we're trying to work here, uh as much as we can.

The radio lit up with chatter. Callsigns, codes, coordinates. Mustang. Gaunt Rays. Niner Niner. Our ears learned to filter the noise, catching only the necessary threads. The camp: Duc Phuong, near the Cambodian border.

One of the two navigators handled initial radio contact with the Ground Controller, callsign "Nifty Tanks." We were finally within striking distance of the camp. Misty Tanks informed us that our ground contact's callsign was "Gaunt Rays," and advised us to contact him once we got close to Duc Phuong.

"Crew Stations," Col Mack ordered.

"Bravo Gunner, ready," I said.

"Alpha Gunner, ready," Barry replied.

We were starting to pick up radio chatter from Gaunt Rays in the Special Forces camp and the nearby artillery company, callsign Niner-Niner.

As we drew near our target area, the navigator briefed emergency procedures. High ground,

Fallback options, crash sites. Jungle all around.

"Gunners go to pre-target checklist," the pilot barked.

The guns were near pre-target status already, so all Barry and I had to do was connect the electrical harnesses to the gun system and remove the mechanical device that ensured the gun couldn't fire.

Barry moved to the rear, scanning for groundfire. I manned the gun control panel. Switches ready. Safeties on. My hands moved without thought, muscle memory guiding them.

Tension built as radio traffic escalated.

Barry, having flown many missions on the AC-47 Spooky, has extensive experience in spotting ground fire.

My position was at the gun control panel, where I responded to the pilot's directions, such as guns HOT (switches set to ARM position) or guns COLD (SAFE). I also changed the rate of fire to the pilot's requests.

The HI rate was 6,000 shots per minute; the LOW rate 3,000. At HI rate, the guns could empty their 1500 round magazines in 15 seconds. I managed the flow of our gunfire.

As each gun depleted its ammo, I enabled the next available gun. I would reload my numbers 1 and 2 guns, and Barry reloaded numbers 3 and 4.

Once we got into a rhythm, we provided the pilot with almost seamless firepower.

It's showtime, baby!

Throughout the remainder of the battle, Nifty Tanks is "Mustang" and Gaunt Rays is "Ski".

Breaking the momentary silence, Ski said, I don't have enough light on my North wall, and that's where they're coming.

Mustang to 62,

Look here, buddy, you're probably coming in from uh Bravo Hotel (Bien Hoa Air Base, near Saigon), so you're coming in from our Southwest. Now, when you come in, pull over the East Side, come up the east side of the runway, and start burning the goddamn wire, buddy. Right at the edge of the runway, and uh, our man, Gaunt Rays, will guide you from there.

Our pilot said, "We're about five miles away now." I'm clear, brother, as well.

Ski contacted us in a panicked voice; I have them coming in from my Echo and from my November.

I have a gate on my Echo leading off the runway, and you can probably see the road. That's where Charlie's at; he's putting satchel charges in the wire and coming in again. I need it right in my wire, right on the edge of it if you can do that for me, please.

Gunfire crackled in the background. Screams echoed through the ether.

62 - Roger, we'll be there in three minutes. We're coming in.

Ski – Roger that, babe, I'm hanging onto my jockstrap right now, it's about the same as I told you before; they still haven't gotten all the way through the wire.

62 – We're coming in from the Echo.

Mustang to Niner Niner – "Flares, baby, flares, flares, just fling one in there!" (Aerial illumination flares)

62 asked Mustang – What's your artillery's Max Ord (highest firing altitude)? We don't want to get hit on our way in.

Mustang says – 3000, but I'll hold my guns until you get set up. You let me know when you're on station. I can hold my guns here, but I hate to hold them because they're holding down the brunt of the attack.

Ski screams into his microphone – I need flares!

Barry was at his station, on the lookout for groundfire, and I was at my control panel, ready to rock and roll. Jenkins, our IO (Illuminator Operator, who operated our illumination flare launcher and our large searchlight), had all his systems online.

My muscles tensed up as we entered our target area. Adrenaline surged through my body, and we were ready to go!

Flare light illuminated the camp. The runway ran north to south. To the west was the camp's west wall, protected by a stretch of barbed wire. The stench of phosphorus permeated the night air.

Ski, contacts Shadow.

"Shadow, let me give you a sitrep before you shoot anything in my wire at this time. How copy?"

Mustang breaks in. We're not gonna be shooting anything in your wire. We're gonna shoot it in our wire, when it's time to shoot it. I wanna get Shadow up here, working to bust this son of a bitch up. You got it, Shadow 62?

Ski says— I'm just waiting for him to get on station; I've got plenty of work for him.

Ski to 62— Ok babe, things have slowed down, I think we hurt Charlie. I see some bad guys hanging in the wire out there at this time.

Ski to 62-- I think what we're going to do, at the Echo and to the November, on my wall, and on my airstrip, and there's a big field to my November. That's generally where Charlie's been moving down from. Could you spray it for me please?

Before 62 could respond, a plaintive cry was heard. We're receiving fire at coordinates 447-0502. Can you check that out, over?

Mustang tells the source— We're tied up in our own battle right now. Then he returns to his conversation with Ski. Just keep your boys down, he'll (62) take care of you; you know I can't talk to you right now. Contact Shadow 62; he'll be up there with it, okay.

Mustang redirects to 62 – Just get up there and start squirting, he'll adjust you. Mack starts his firing pass and alerts Ski, okay, here comes some rounds, let me know how they look.

Mack rolls the big black beast into a left-hand bank, setting up a firing orbit. "Gunner, guns Hot, one gun, the pilot commands. Guns Hot! I confirm."

I hit the switch. Gun #1 spun to life, a roaring chainsaw, spitting flame into the jungle.

Burning red tracers, snakelike, lick their way through the battlefield in search of their prey.

Ski to 62, "That looks good, babe, bring it over to my West wall, that's where they're coming in from, about 800 meters Whiskey."

"Ok, here comes 6 thou (6,000 rounds)," 62 responded.

Gun #1 ran dry in mere minutes. I switched to #3 for Barry, then reloaded it. We are in rhythm now, and we are in for some work tonight.

Hot brass.
Cool nerves.
Burning sky.

Shadow has arrived,
and hell followed close behind.

Chapter 2
Speed is Life

It was a clandestine mission over the Ho Chi Minh Trail, and a secretive gunship had located its prey, NVA trucks.

The moonless night offered good conditions for
attacking a group of enemy trucks hiding beneath the jungle canopy.

As the gunship pilot rolled into a left-hand bank, the IO frantically called out, "Pilot, IO, AAA, 6 o'clock, highly accurate, break left, break left!"

The pilot quickly increased his roll to evade the AAA. "Break left, hard! It's going to hit!" The enemy gunner was dialed in to the gunship's path.

The burst of enemy rounds narrowly missed the gunship, but its wings unexpectedly rolled full vertical.

Lift: gone—control: lost.

The pilot attempted to regain control, but the plane continued rolling until it was eventually upside down.

Rear cabin crew and unsecured items were hurled to the ceiling. Ammo cans and gear became lethal missiles, and men scrambled for cover.

Luckily, their parachute packs detached from their hangers and were easily accessible.

They struggled to don their parachutes after the pilot commanded them to prepare to abandon the aircraft upon hearing the bell.

The pilot told the IO, "Do not jettison the flare launcher. "It could be a danger to crew members abandoning the aircraft."

To increase air speed, the pilot and copilot lowered the aircraft's nose and initiated a descent toward the ground.

As the nose lowered, the aircraft transitioned from upside-down to vertical orientation. The rear crew desperately clung to internal structures to avoid falling towards the forward bulkhead, which was now 40 feet below them.

Key issues included not only a loss of control but also minimal visibility due to the darkness.

Surrounded by jagged karst terrain and towering rocky cliffs, the plane once again came under anti-aircraft fire, rapidly losing altitude as it plunged toward the ground upside down.

Despite the low altitude, the pilot and copilot successfully regained control of the aircraft, pulling it out of the inverted loop, and back to normal flight attitude.

The crew and aircraft endured g-forces that the Korean War vintage cargo plane had not been designed for.

Disoriented, the pilot risked turning on his wing landing lights to check his proximity to the karst. This disclosed his position to enemy gunners.

As a visual scan revealed the plane was clear of the karst, he quickly switched off the lights. However, it was in a narrow valley, heading back to dangerous territory.

Inverted flight damaged their instruments and scattered maps. To return home, they needed to exit the valley and move beyond the AAA range.

The pilot contacted the IO: "Can you get the illuminator running?" The IO replied, "I'll try," and soon after confirmed, "It's up and running, sir."

The pilot directed the IO to set the illuminator to the narrowest beam, IR filter, and full depression.

The IO confirmed, all set. What's next, sir?

I want you to, on my command, go to white light and slowly scan upwards to max elevation. Be ready to shut her off as soon as possible.

Got it, sir. Ready to go.

The pilot said, "We need to check the height of the karst on the left to determine if we have enough clearance to climb and turn left toward home. We're too beat up to risk tangling with that AAA again."

The pilot called out, "Light on!" As the IO toggled his controls from IR to White, the narrow white beam pierced the night sky, probing the jagged karst.

As the IO guided the light upwards to its limit, the pilot called back, saying, "IO, I got it, shut'er down." "Roger, pilot, shutting down."

The pilot guided the plane up and over the karst, performed a sharp left turn, and proceeded toward home base.

After moving beyond enemy artillery, the navigator received guidance from the Airborne Command Center. The navigator then charted a return course while the crew secured equipment that had moved during earlier maneuvers. The crew began their journey back following an eventful night.

Except for minor bumps and bruises, the crew suffered no injuries. They would all have an amazing story to share upon their return home.

Chapter 3
The Battle Continues

Shadow 62, this is Ski, could you bring it in a little tighter, closer to my camp? Ok, we'll bring it closer.

Shadow, get it out there, they're coming in through my wire! You're too far to my November! Bring it south about 200 meters! Moments later, Ski responds in panic, they're in my perimeter, Shadow, they're in my perimeter, babe! I've got to have it on my wire!

Mustang breaks in, Ski, get down in the hole, Ski says I ain't gotta hole, Tom!

Mustang redirects to Shadow. Put it on his wire, just inside his camp! Before Shadow can respond, Ski yells, On my west wall! That's where they're coming in. I need it on my west wall, and hurry!

Amid the cacophony of automatic weapon fire and people screaming, Mustang breaks in again, Shadow, put it on his west wall or the man's had it!

A torrent of red tracers sped toward the west wall, feverishly searching for their targets.

Ski says to Shadow, you're looking good, babe. You come any closer; you'll get me.
Barry and I were now in maximum overdrive, maintaining the flow of hot lead. Col Mack responds, Here comes six thou!

Ski corrects Shadow's fire. Put it on that red water tower with the black shit on it.
Mustang chimes in, Sock it to 'em buddy, they're in the hole and Charlies in there with 'em.

Ski affirms to Shadow, that's looking real good. Amid the radio chatter comes a notification from Mustang that there's a section of Blue Max, Army attack helicopters, on the way.

Mustang directs another controller, call sign Mexican, to take over communication with the section of Blue Maxes on radio frequency 49.35.

Once the Blue Maxes arrive, our combined firepower should be able to quell this attack.

What began as a heated skirmish has evolved into an all-out battle to save the camp and the souls therein.

We are rapidly burning through our 33,000 rounds of ammunition. Barely two hours after wheels up, and we're almost out of ammo.

As we pass over the camp in our attacks, the IO drops an illumination flare. We only carry 24, so we'll also run out of flares. Our backup is our powerful, 1 million lumen searchlight.

Mustang asks Shadow, Can we get another Shadow up here? One of the navigators chimes in that he'll make the call.

Meanwhile, Ski redirects Shadow's fire to his West wall, that's where Charlie's coming in from.

The battle evolves into a deadly version of Whack-A-Mole, with the gunship responding to Ski's rapidly changing directions, valiantly working to turn the tide of the fight.

Col Mack, a highly experienced Command Pilot, wheels the big gunship around the skies as easily as he would a little Cessna.

He sends another ribbon of death earthward. Ski responds, You're looking good, babe, you're choppin' 'em up! Quickly, Ski followed with a plea to keep the rounds outside the camp, as he is sending in a platoon to relieve an embattled platoon at the perimeter.

Barry and I are working at a fever pitch now. One of the navigators comes back to help by shuffling ammo cans of spent brass and links out of our way so we can focus our energy on maintaining devastating firepower.

Meanwhile, as the gunship performed its deadly dance among the aerial flares, the radio crackles to life with the voices of Mexican and Max 47 Hotel.

Max this is Mexican. We need you to run South to North and fire your rockets up the East side of the runway. After that, we need your miniguns along the perimeter until you reach the West Wall. How copy?

47 Hotel Copy, starting my run now, correct my fire as needed.

Shadow, this is Mustang. I need you to cease fire and pull off to the East while Max does his runs. Copy all, said Shadow.

Pulling off target for a bit gave Barry and me a breather, allowing us to watch the show below. It was quite a show, as the Helicopter gunships launched a barrage of rockets into the runway's Eastern flank.

The rockets appeared similar to fireworks whose path was horizontal.

Their impacts exploded with showers of sparks and flames. The rockets were also armed with flechette warheads.

Flechettes were a devastating anti-personnel weapon that launched thousands of four-inch steel arrows at the enemy.

From our gunports, we could see the effects through the smoke and haze, illuminated by flickering flare light. Groups of enemy soldiers were struck down where they stood, as if by giant hands.

After-action reports of our missions typically stated that each enemy soldier had been struck by at least a dozen of our rounds. Horrific as that was, it paled in comparison to the destruction wrought by the flechette rockets.

But the enemy kept coming, wave after wave, placing satchel charges in the wire as they stormed the compound.

Like crazed zombies, the NVA soldiers made desperate advances through the perimeter's barbed wire, using their fallen brethren as stair steps over the barbed wire.

It was a scene burned into our minds forever, as a reminder of the barbaric brutality of war.

We rarely had the chance to be observers.

The numbers on the body count board in our Operations building were sobering reminders of the toll we exacted on the enemy.

Each night, our flight launched at least four to five missions, with a nightly average of hundreds of enemy soldiers meeting their fate from these missions.

The Blue Maxes expended their ordnance, launching their final rounds at the West Wall as they departed for their home base.

Ski broke up the show, requesting we return to the West Wall. We advised him that we were running low on ammo and only had 9 flares left.

We were orbiting East of the camp, so we had to swing around towards the West Wall. As we made our turn, a new voice, Smoky Three, came up on the radio. Mustang, this is Smokey Three. Can I get a sitrep?

Smokey Three is a USAF Forward Air Controller, launched by the Airborne Command Post, as an on-scene director.

Smokey Three, we have our little A-camp out here getting the shit kicked out of them, said Mustang.

We have Shadow above, kicking out flares and minigun fire, he continued.

The Blue Maxes have just departed, and there's another section on its way.

My artillery is out of flares; Shadow is down to nine flares, and he's using his big flashlight for illume.

We have another Shadow on the way, and we've requested Tac Air with Napalm and CBUs.

Smokey Three said, I have a Moonshine flare ship on its way that's ten minutes out. It'll provide you with all night light.

I'm here to coordinate Tac Air. It's on the way, don't worry, we'll take care of you.

Satchel charges. Blue Maxes. Shadows. flechettes—stark instruments of war's brutality.

North Vietnam was not a signatory to the Geneva Convention.

The VC and NVA waged war with extreme malice, intentionally targeting American and South Vietnamese medics, ambulances, and medivac helicopters, acts devoid of honor.

Without a formal declaration of war, the North justified its brutal treatment of POWs, captured airmen, and soldiers, claiming they were not combatants but terrorists.

Chapter 4
Weasels and Jollies

We depended on rescue units to get us out of harm's way if we were shot down or crashed. Rescue teams and the Wild Weasel aircrews were among the most heroic groups during the Vietnam War.

Wild Weasels were tasked to fly one of the war's most dangerous missions, SAM suppression. Faced with flying ahead of a group of fighter-bombers, the Weasels would entice enemy SAM sites into turning on their radars so the Weasels could launch a missile to destroy them. Initial reaction from the first Wild Weasel aircrews, "You gotta be shitting me," shortened to YGBSM.

Jollies were the rescue squadrons' helicopter assets.
Flying into the most perilous conditions, Jollies were tasked with extracting downed aircrews. Slow-moving, they hovered over a downed airman, becoming excellent targets for enemy soldiers.

The pararescue team retrieved the airmen, treating their injuries as they sped away to safety.

Their only protection was provided by a gunner and a Sandy (propeller-driven fighter) overhead.

Shootdown of Jolly 71

The following is a transcription of a 9-minute recording of the actual event, transcribed as accurately as possible.

... Over here, One-nine (Jolly 19). They're turning about 265, 050 for 67 miles.

I can't tell them, this is 77, base plus 78. Over here. What are we to you? We sure crossed over the border.

One-nine, King 3, what position are we? What clock are you from us? All right, we haven't got anything. I think I've got you now.

Okay, you should be 12 o'clock to him. Roger. Roger, roger, copy.

All right, let's see what we've got. Okay, anything with an AIM-7 or an AIM-4, we'd appreciate it.

Anything with a what? AIM-7 or an AIM-4. (AIM-7 and AIM-4 are air-to-air missiles; the audio doesn't explain why missiles entered into the discussion).

They may have been discussing MigCAP (missile-armed Fighter Protection).

Okay, if you can slow it up to about 80 knots or something like that, so I can catch you now, I'm going to leave you behind. Roger, Roger. Okay, I'll be at 8,000, about 20.

Roger. 10-degree arc. So, we've been over the fence? Oh, probably three or four times already.

That soundly is well within the border. All right, that's a good 10 miles on it. That was the one I was worried about having to cross.

Yeah, that's got a main railroad in it, hey, look at the rocket! Holy Christ.

Go down, go down.

Okay, would you come by so I can be ready so we can diagonal? 89. 89. All right.

And we'll try to take 2,000 again. Okay.

Watch those Migs.

Watch for chutes. There's the Migs. There's no chute.

He's done. Get down. Migs, Migs.

Jolly Green 71's been hit. Guys, get down choppers. Migs, Migs.

10-3. 10-3. 10-3.

Where's that fire at? Right at this group here? That's a Charlie. I'm not too sure which one it was. It was either 70, 77, 71, or 72 that blew up in that air out here.

Hey, that 70 was just wiped out. He was just knocked completely out of the air. No chutes.

Zigzag, man. Zigzag. Let's get down.

Okay, let's vacate this area, gang. Watch for the Migs. You see anything looking toward us, let me know.

That was a rocket.

71 was wiped out with a Mig. My God.

Chutes wiped out. Guys, get down. Let's get in the tree tops, boys.

Get down on the deck. Mayday, Mayday, Sandy 5 on Guard. We have a big Jolly down, 050 for 63.

Looks like it was hit midair by either a Mig or a missile. That was a Mig with a rocket. 72 is here.

It passed me, got 70. Wiped him out. Go that way, sir.

Where's the Mig now? Make a right turn, pull up. Get down on the deck.

I advise all choppers, get on that deck. Head west. Behind this hill here for a minute.

Okay. Okay, King, we're going down on the deck. We're RTB.

We copy that. Get down. Roger, Roger.

Get down on the deck and stay there. 19, Sandy 4 is right behind. Go ahead and down.

Roger that. Anything west from behind, west to the right. West.

We can see ahead. Keep up. Sandy here, do you see any of those Migs? I'm sitting like a duck out here.

Goddamn, they were. King, do you read 72? Roger. That was a Mig.

He passed me. The rocket went past to my right and hit 70. He was a ball of flame. I dodged the debris.

We watched for chutes. There couldn't have possibly been any survivors out of that one.

Roger. Let's get the fuck out of here. 72 is RTB, and we're heading at a heading of 240.

We're on the deck. Okay, get down. Let's get down a little lower.

All Jollies get on the deck. Get on the deck, Sandy. 7 o'clock.

7 o'clock. Zigzag. I think that was it.

Okay, gang, 210 looks like a pretty good heading, Navigator says. Pretty good heading for 72. Say again.

210, 72, 210. That's left. Roger, 210.

Do we have a Mig cap now? I've got one ordered. Thanks a lot. Aw Shit.

70 is wiped out completely. 71. Correction, 71.

That was my best friend in the room. Keep watching to the right and let me know if you see anything. Roger.

We've got an aircraft at 3 o'clock, but it looks like Sandy. Sandy at 3 o'clock. We've got a Sandy at 9 o'clock.

I could hear that explosion. Ah shit, me too. I saw the rocket.

I saw the jet come by. I saw the rocket. The next thing followed.

It wasn't 50 feet off to the right. What? I had a search. It wasn't 50 feet off to the right.

I said that one that went by us. I thought it was going to be to the right. That was a MiG-21, by the way, in case you want to make a note of it.

I saw it. It was Sandy-5. I had a dirt tank through here.

It was Sandy-5. We've got weapons at 6 o'clock, give us some cover.

There's a MiG over there. There's a MiG at 9 o'clock. MiG at 9 o'clock.

It's going over the top of the hill. Sandy at our 9 o'clock position, he's coming our way.

I got him. He's coming back on us, too. I'll tell you, Van, I think maybe we'd better head for a valley here or something. He's pulling up. Don't come this way, Tom, watch it, keep him in sight.

He's coming over the top. That's an F-4. Is that an F-4? I'll take that 72.

Do you have an F-4 in the area? He's at our 6 o'clock position right now. Let's just walk up over the top of this hill and down around the... ...ground. Got him in sight. Roger.

Is he coming our way? Looks like he's going away from us. Let's hide down here a minute. There's a village down here at 6 o'clock.

Well, shit, we're going to have to go up, then. I know.

King, this is 72. Do you read?

End of recording.

Incident Details

28 January 1970
Jolly Green 71   Seabird 02
40th ARRS   44TFS,355TFW
HH-53B # 66-14434   F-105G 63-8329

Jolly Green 71 was shot down by a Vietnamese Air Force MiG-21 while attempting to rescue crewmen from a downed F-105 Thunderchief in North Vietnam.

It was January 28, 1970, Captains Richard J. Mallon, pilot, and Robert J. Panek, Sr., EWO, aboard an F-105G Wild Weasel, call sign Seabird 02, departed Udorn Airfield as the second aircraft in a flight of two conducting a SAM suppression mission to locate and destroy surface-to-air missile (SAM) sites near Nui Dai Ninh, Ha Tinh Province, North Vietnam.

Seabird flight was escorting an RF-4C on a photo-reconnaissance mission over North Vietnam.

The mission identifiers were Steel Tiger, Cricket Area 4. The location featured rugged forested mountains, home to large concentrations of NVA troops.

Situated 20 miles northeast of the Mu Gia Pass, it was one of the two major entry points into the Ho Chi Minh Trail.

Upon arrival of Seabird flight in the target area, Seabird 01 established radio contact with the airborne battlefield command and control center (ABCCC), controlling all air operations in this region, for last-minute instructions.

The ABCCC then handed Seabird flight over to the on-site forward air controller (FAC), directly in charge of this flight.

The FAC cleared Seabird flight into the target area for the search for SAM sites located along Route 15, the primary road running through the Mu Gia Pass.

Seabird 01 pressed forward, flying low over the countryside, trolling enemy gunners to turn on their radars before they launched SAMs at him.

Seabird 02 remained high, prepared to strike the SAM site once it obtained a lock on the enemy radar. It was a dangerous tactic for the air crews, as they intentionally exposed themselves to enemy gunners.

Seabird 01 identified an active SAM site, and as Seabird 02 attacked it, it was struck by an air-to-air missile from a MiG-21, assigned to the North Vietnamese Air Force's 921st Flight Regiment.

Seabird 02's crew was forced to eject from their crippled Thunderchief. Observers saw both parachutes deployed and heard two emergency radio beepers from the survivors, but no voice contact could be established with either.

Seabird 01 immediately requested that a search and rescue (SAR) mission be initiated.

Within minutes, the rescue force, including two HH-53B rescue helicopters, was dispatched from Udorn Airfield, Thailand, to pick up Seabird 02's crew.

Seabird 02's crash site was in a 50-foot wide open area, straddled by the Rau Cai River to the west and Route 15 to the east. Twelve miles east of the North Vietnamese/Lao border and 17 miles north-northeast of Mu Gia Pass, it was also 53 miles northwest of Dong Hoi and 61 miles south of Vinh.

Once the rescue force arrived in the target area, the FAC directed them into a holding area located approximately 23 miles northwest of the downed Wild Weasel air crew.

As Jolly Green 71 awaited clearance from the FAC to enter the rescue area, the HH-53B rescue helicopter was attacked and shot down by an Atoll air-to-air missile from a second MiG-21, piloted by Vu Ngoc Dinh, a

North Vietnamese ace of the 921st Flight Regiment, with 6 kills to his credit.

Air crews in the vicinity watched in horror as the MiG-21 attacked the helicopter, causing it to explode in a fireball, turning the rescue helicopter into hundreds of pieces of burning debris that fell onto the steep mountainside.

A brief beeper signal was heard from the crash site, raising hopes that there might have been one survivor, but none were located. At the time of loss, all six men were immediately listed as Missing in Action.

Jolly Green 71's crash site was rugged, heavily forested, and approximately ½ mile east of the North Vietnamese/Lao border.

It was 10 miles west of Route 15, 23 miles northwest of Seabird 02's loss location, 38 miles south-southwest of Vinh, and 83 miles northwest of Dong Hoi.

By the end of the hostilities, Jolly 71 was the only Jolly Green helicopter shot down due to air-to-air action.

Please acknowledge the sacrifice of these six men aboard Jolly 71, struck down amid their calling to serve:

"That others may live."

Major Holly G. Bell

Capt. Leonard C. Leeser

SSgt. William C. Shinn

MSgt. William C. Sutton

SMSgt. William D. Pruet

SSgt. Gregory L. Anderson

Major Holly G. Bell
Pilot

Capt. Leonard C. Leeser
Co-pilot

SMSgt. William D. Pruett
Pararescueman

SSgt. William C. Shinn
Flight Engineer

MSgt. William C. Sutton
Pararescueman

Sgt. Gregory L. Anderson
Combat Photographer

And, not to be forgotten, the crew of F-105G Seabird 02, who ejected and survived, only to be executed by the North Vietnamese militia near the crash site.

Captains Richard J. Mallon, Pilot, and Robert J. Panek, Sr., EWO.

Capt. Richard J. Mallon Capt. Robert J Panek Sr
Pilot   EWO

Chapter 5
The Battle Rages on

Smokey 3, this is Mustang. "Where are your jets?"
"They're not here yet," said Smokey 3.

Ski tells Shadow to keep up the illumination.

Mustang continues, "Smokey 3, I understand you've got one set of jets with hard bombs. When they get here, I need them to rip apart the west side, about 300 meters from his wire. Smoky 3 confirms, 300 meters from the FOB."

Mustang directs Smokey 3. "When the napalm and CBU's get here, you can put them right in the wire." "Okay, you talk to Ski right now! He's up in the A-camp, in bad shape."

"Okay, Ski, talk to Smokey 3, he's got hard bombs, jets, nape, and CBU's coming up!"

Ski in a panic, screams, "Shadow, I need some of that gunfire on my east, they're coming back in there!"

Mustang assures Ski that we'll kill every one of these motherfuckers!
Mustang says, "Shadow put some of your goddam fire on the east side of the camp, buddy. How copy?" Shadow says, "Copy, we're going over there now."

Meanwhile, Blue Maxes are making minigun runs along the east side. Ski encourages the Blue Maxes, "Beautiful, you're looking good babe."

Shadow begins hosing down the east side of the runway. On board the gunship, a discussion ensues about where to put our fire, the scope operator confirms to the pilot that our fire needs to be right on the east wire.

It is only a moment's break, but Barry and I continue to reload our guns.

Pilot comes up on intercom, I haven't got a gun!

Barry and I feverishly check gun status. I've given the pilot a gun twice, to no avail! Not a good situation. Barry reports, we've given you two guns, and the pilot responds that he's pushing his trigger!

As if by magic, one of the miniguns spins up in an angry roar, spewing hot lead and tracers down to the camp's east wire.

The show continues, thank goodness.

Mustang breaks in, telling Shadow to drop a flare every time they go over the A-camp.

Mustang adds, "Shadow, run your fire up and down the east side of the runway. There are about eight million of those motherfuckers over there. Shadow responds, we'll get 'em all!"

Shadow, this is Mustang. "What's your situation on ordinance? We're checking now."

Barry does a quick count of the remaining ammo, reporting the total to Col. Mack, who advises Mustang: "We've got eight thousand rounds left."

Col. Mack has really been keeping Barry and me humping in the back.

Mustang advises Shadow to keep dropping flares and hold off those eight thousand rounds till we need them. We only have a few flares left, artillery-wise.

Smokey 3, this is Mustang. "Where's that damn flare ship? It's on the way; it'll be here soon."

Ski once again screams to Shadow, "They're coming in on my north, I need that fire right on top of my bunkers!"
Shadow, "I can't observe your fire, but keep it on my bunkers. I've got my people down."
Suddenly, Max 48 India comes up on the radio, requesting a situation report.

Ski tells him to put his miniguns on his bunkers and his rockets on his north wall.

Mustang, this is Shadow 62. "We've got Shadow 78 on his way in with 30,000 rounds, about ten minutes out."

Mustang tells Shadow 62, to give 78 a sitrep when he gets in, and we'll use those 30,000 rounds.

Meanwhile Max 48 India, Mustang, Ski and Smokey 3 are embroiled in a heated exchange.

Frustrations are running high, as 48 India is insisting on a marker light on the ground to identify the "Target."

Mustang finally jumps in and says to Ski, "Just give the man (48 India) a fuckin' light, even if you have to light your cigarette lighter."

Mustang to 48 India, "Max, buddy, just talk to Ski, he's in bad shape, half his camp is lost, he's got nobody outside his wire, just take his direction and start shooting, he'll adjust you."

Max, this is Ski, "I'm going to put a flare right in the center of the fucking camp. What I want you to do, I want you to make your run from east to west on my north wall, I want you to put miniguns on top of the bunkers, and rockets in that fuckin' wall and hurry!"

48 India says, "I'm about 02/03 out. Ski says, let me know when you get over my location, and I'll blow this flare for you."

Shadow contacts 48 India. "I'm orbiting over the camp, I've just run out of ammo and I've got my big flashlight on. He wants you to pulverize the north side of the camp from the bunkers out to the wire.
We'll stay here and illuminate with our white light; we have another gunship right behind us."

Ski tells Shadow, "Hold your minigun off the top of my bunkers. We got holes in the roof, and the shit was coming in through the holes."

"Put it close to those bunkers, without putting it on top of them, that's what I need."

"You're doing an outstanding job. I love you all to death."

Major Williams, our Co-pilot, calls back to Jenkins to launch one of our two remaining flares. Jenkins says "Flare away!"
Moments later the flares' parachute is ejected, and the illumination charge ignites, casting an intense yellowish light over the beleaguered camp.

Mustang engages Ski again, as the jets with hard bombs have almost arrived. "Outside your wire, about 300 meters, we'll drop hard bombs and then use the napalm and CBU's in the wire when they get here."

Ski says "It sounds like a Betty Crocker Cookbook, and I need it!"

Mustang says, "Okay, there's a bunch of motherfuckers on the east side, and laying all over the runway."

Mustang tells Shadow to kick out his last flare, Shadow responds that they kicked it out a minute ago. Mustang adds that we have a Moonshine Flare ship on its way, and he'll be up here just in a minute.

Ski tells Shadow that the white light's doing me some good, it lets my people pick off the bad guys. Shadow says he'll keep the light on him.

Mustang tells 99er, get ready with your remaining flares and to fire when Shadow's flare goes out.

Parachute flares, artillery flares, searchlights, cigarette lighters. The night, once the enemy's domain, is now lost.

Brass

We shoot da guns
We fix da guns
We load da guns
We sling da brass
We shovel da brass
Brass, brass
Everywhere brass
Shoot it, shovel it
Load it, sling it
Gunners are we
It's what we do

--Jim Mattison
  Aerial Gunner --

As the light from Shadow's flare diminishes to a flicker, 99er fires his remaining artillery flares.

The artillery flares only last about a minute, whereas Shadow's flares last over three minutes.

Mustang, Ski and 99er express panic that Shadow's out of flares, 99er is almost out of his flares, when a welcome voice comes up on the radio, "Mustang, this is Smoky 3, I now have the flare ship over your camp. Contact Moonshine on this frequency and tell him where you want the light."

A jubilant Mustang asks Moonshine what his flare status is. Moonshine responds that, "Launching two at a time, I have enough flares for about three hours."

Huzzah! This will cover the camp well beyond sunup.

Smokey 3 says "I've got my jets holding a few clicks (kilometers) out from your camp. They're ready to work. Where do you want their ordnance?"

Mustang says, "Put your hard bombs parallel to the camp's west wire, about 300 meters out. Gimme a holler when they start their run, so we can keep our boys down! Smokey 3 says 10-4, they'll start their run in 03, I'll throw a smoke rocket into the west wire as a marker they can see. The smoke will glow from the flare light above."

Ski, "Get your boys down, the jets are making their run. Mustang, we're all in bunkers, no sweat. We're just waiting for the show."

As soon as Ski released the button on his radio microphone, his west wire erupted with the fury of a hundred volcanos. The ground shook as if a runaway freight train passed through the camp. Fragments from the explosive iron cut down trees and brush like giant weed whackers.

Smokey 3 breaks in, asking Mustang, "How'd that look, buddy?"

Mustang says "Real good, real good. How about another run 100 meters further out? You'll kill more of those bastards trying to get away."

Smokey 3 announces he'll put another marker rocket in for confirmation and then send the jets in again.

Ski tells Smokey 3, "I got my people down, your smoke looks good, let'em have it!"

"Okey, dokey, says Smoky 3, one order of hell coming right up! Hang onto your jock straps, my jets are on their way in."

Further out from the camp, an earthquake hit as the jets released their bombs. Once again, explosive fury engulfed the enemy soldiers attempting to escape the devastation.

Meanwhile, Shadow 78 has just arrived, taking up an orbit 180 degrees out from Shadow 62's orbit. The two gunships performed an eerie ballet amid the yellow flare light, diffused by the smoke-filled night sky.

A sky that, on any other night, would be pitch black, save the stars overhead.

With their situation briefing completed, Shadow 62 contacted Ski and Mustang. "We've briefed Shadow 78 on your situation; he's got 33,000 rounds of ammo and 24 flares at your disposal. We are Winchester on ammo and nearing Bingo fuel, so we've got to RTB for the night."

"It was our pleasure to assist you boys. Feel free to call Shadow again when you need some help."

Ski chimed in, "Shadow, you've done a marvelous job, saving our bacon tonight." Mustang says "Roger that Ski", "Shadow 62, if you hadn't arrived, our little camp out here wouldn't have survived! This has been one hell of an attack we've had tonight, and you've done a fine job of keeping those little mothers on the run."

"Thank you all. We're out of here. Please get in touch with Shadow 78 on this frequency. We've passed the baton, and he'll take care of you. Shadow 62 out."

Smokey 3 adds, "Thanks for being here Shadow 62, you've done an amazing job taking care of these guys, but we've come to expect that from Shadow."

Smokey 3 says to Mustang, "My jets are RTB, and more are coming.' My jets with the CBUs and Nape are holding about 10 clicks out."

"They're picking up some heavy small arms fire, and they're telling me there's a 51 Cal out there giving them fits. Is it okay with you if I have Shadow 78 go over there and deal with the AAA?"

Mustang responds that he approves of the diversion. Skis' people are cleaning up a bit after the beating Charlie's taken. We're not sure if Charlie will regroup and try again. I need that Shadow handy.

Mustang continues, "When I give you the go-ahead, first, I need the CBU on the east side of the runway about 100 meters east, from north to south. I need the Nape about 100 meters east of where you put the CBU.

Then I want you to hold your jets away from the camp while we see where we need the rest of their ordnance.

Smokey 3 responds that he'll go with the plan.

Chapter 6
Scramble!

Location: Nha Trang AB, RVN, 71st SOS
Operations Building
Time: 1800
Mission: Shadow 60, Ground Alert
Crew: Crew 11, AC Capt. Bob Wisner

The final rays of today's sun, scattered
through the Southeast Asia haze, caused a
radiant orange glow emanating from the city
of Nha Trang.

Crew 11 had already pre-flighted and
readied their gunship to launch at a
moment's notice.

Most of the officers were relaxing in the
ready room, some reading the Stars and
Stripes newspaper, while others watched
Armed Forces Radio and TV on the black-
and-white TV.

The FE, Tsgt Kirby and the IO Sgt Fuentes
had gone outside to have a smoke.

The gunners, Sgts Blanchard and Short
were engaged in a rousing game of Spades.

Usually quiet until darkness fell, the crew enjoyed the few moments of relaxation. At least as much as they could relax, knowing that things could change at any moment with a blast on the klaxon, signaling they were being scrambled into action.

As darkness overcame the giant airbase, Kirby and Fuentes could be seen pitching horseshoes under the dim floodlights behind the Ops Building.

The two men halted their game and listened to the familiar "kachunk, kachunk" sound of mortar fire. Kirby says, "I wonder what the Security Teams have stirred up? They probably have Charlie probing the perimeter."

Minutes later, the whoosh and boom of a possible rocket pierced the normally quiet evening.

Kirby says to Fuentes, "I think we'd better get inside and prepare for a klaxon."

Almost as soon as they stepped inside Ops, the base sirens began their haunting wail, followed by the klaxon signaling they were being launched.

The night shift admin clerk served as the crew bus driver. The bus was actually just a pickup truck with two benches in the bed. He was already outside with the truck running, awaiting his passengers.

It was a short hop to the Alert Shadow. He delivered his passengers and hurried back to the Ops building.

As the crew boarded the gunship, the Crew Chief already had aircraft power applied. The crew approached their stations and did quick checks, confirming they were ready to roll.

After the engines started and a quick check by the flight crew, the crew chief pulled the chocks, and the gunship taxied out towards the end of the runway.

Communication with the tower and DASC revealed the gunship was being scrambled for air base defense.

For maximum readiness, Capt. Wisner commanded the crew to go to immediate pre-target condition. The gunners made all four miniguns ready for battle, and the IO fired up the Illuminator and readied the Flare Launcher for action.

He swung the big gunship around the end of the runway and lined up on the centerline. As a final check, he ran the engines up to maximum power and held them there.

He asked the FE, "How's she look? Is she ready to go?" The FE made a quick scan of the engine gauges and proclaimed, "She's ready to go!"

The pilot released the brakes, and with full takeoff power, the big plane lurched forward, making its way down the runway.

With a mighty heave and groan, the gunship finally leaped from the safety of Terra Firma into the night, with only the dim lighting of the air base below.

Once airborne, Shadow 60 was directed to enter a holding pattern near Hong Tre Island.

Hong Tre was an island in Nha Trang Bay, and a favorite haven for the Viet Cong.

Many attacks emanated from the island due to its proximity to the air base. During the day it was a favorite target for the Tactical Fighters and their napalm bombs.

At night, the Viet Cong came out to play, on most nights launching harassing mortar and rocket attacks.

Such was the case tonight. However, there was a difference. Tonight, the VC launched a simultaneous attack of US assets located in town and an attack from Hong Tre.

Shadow's Night Vision Scope would help locate the attackers near the town, and the US Strike Teams could engage the enemy. If directed, Shadow could locate the attacks on the island.

The DASC contacted Shadow and requested that they focus their attention on the town.

The Pilot announced to the crew, "We're going to do something a little different tonight." "Command needs us to find the VC attacking the Consulate and our off-base billets."

"We are not cleared to shoot anything in town, so we're going in as a search team." "I need you guys to act as spotters for our Strike Teams."

"Gunners go Safe on the guns." "IO, I don't think we'll need illume right now, the city's lit up pretty good, so shut the light down for now." "How copy?"

"Pilot, gunner, guns are Safe." "Pilot, IO, Lamps off."

Three sets of eyes and the NOS scanned for enemy activity as the gunship orbited the city.

"Pilot, IO, I think I see some activity, our 8 o'clock, about 150 yards out." "NOS, can you pick that up?"

"This is NOS. I have some troops on the second floor of a hotel." "I'll track so we can get a better look." "Tracking."

Capt. Wisner yawed the plane to the left, lining up his gunsight." "NOS, is that better?"

"Yes, Pilot, I can identify the location. This is the hotel where some of our NCOs are billeted." "It looks like some of the NCOs are being armed up to repel the attackers." "I see some people handing out weapons to the guys standing outside of their rooms."

"Pilot to Nav, contact DASC and advise we have enemy troops threatening our billeting hotel."

DASC advises Shadow 60 that they have a Strike Team on its way.

"Pilot, gunner, I see what looks like automatic weapons fire coming from the Big Buddha, at our 3 o'clock!" Copilot says, "I see tracers from the Buddha, they're firing into the city!"

"Pilot to NAV, contact DASC, advise them we have automatic weapons fire from the Buddha." "Ask if we're cleared to engage?" "Roger, NAV."

"Pilot, NAV, DASCC says we are not, I repeat NOT to engage." "The Buddha is a sensitive location and they are dispatching Police and ARVN to engage."

"DASC to Shadow 60." "Shadow 60 responds, go ahead."

"We need you to head over Hong Tre and see if you can find and neutralize the VC rocket teams." "They're accelerating their barrage."

"Roger, this is Shadow 60, we're heading over there now."

Capt. Wisner says to the crew, "Looks like we might be able to get in some fighting tonight after all." "Gunners, go guns Hot, and give me one gun low rate." "IO, fire up the Illuminator and ready the Flare Launcher."

"Guns Hot, Sir." "IO says, Illuminator coming online, Launchers ready, Sir."

Pilot says, "Ok, boys, let's go find us some VC to kill." "NOS, are you ready? Keep a sharp eye for rocket flashes." "NOS is up."

Hong Tre is a moderately sized island, much like Catalina Island off the coast of California.

Capt. Wisner established a large lazy orbit around the island. One of the gunners helped spot for ground fire.

NOS said, "Pilot, I just spotted a flash in the jungle. I'm tracking for you." "Okay, I got another one for you, nearby."

"Copilot, call DASC and request clearance to fire." "Roger." Said Capt. Phipps.

Moments later, the Copilot says, "We have a clearance. DASC declares this a free-fire zone."

"Pilot says, Ok gunners, looks like we have some work, give me two guns, low rate."

Gunner Blanchard says "Roger pilot, two guns hot, low rate."

Capt. Wisner, "Ok, we're rolling in hot!"

A minute later, after banking the gunship, Capt. Wisner sends down a flurry of hot lead and tracers.

Even as the gunship's deadly fire streaks towards them, the enemy responds with small arms fire. The gunship is high enough for the enemy's fire to be ineffective. The gunship's rounds find their mark, causing small explosions. The NOS says, "Pilot, looks like we got that guy, not sure if it's a mortar tube or a rocket launcher, but we got some secondaries from that first burst."

"Pilot, NOS, the enemy teams were about 20 yards apart. I'll track the explosion site, and you can hose around the area." "We might kill the team or at least damage the tube."

Pilot says, "Roger NOS, here comes another burst."
Suddenly, the pilot exclaims, "What was that?" "I just saw some tracers go past us, but underneath." "Somebody get some eyes on the source, pronto!"

"Pilot, gunner, there's something at our four o'clock shooting at us, looks like a 51 cal." "It's just below that ridgeline."

Capt. Wisner broke from the target, seeking refuge on the other side of the ridge. He said, "We should be safe here, that gun is below the ridge, so he'll only have 180 degrees of coverage."

Pilot to IO, "I have an idea, can you set two flares for max delay?" "I want to punch them out, and when they ignite, hopefully they'll blind the enemy gunners long enough for me to dump a few thousand rounds on them."

"Pilot to IO, when I tell you, launch the two flares." "I'll launch when we're over the tip of the ridge."

Copilot says, "That sounds crazy enough to work." Pilot responds, "Here we go, gunners give me two on high rate!" "IO, launch two flares!" Pilot says, "NOS, if you have the gun's location, track it in case the flares obscure my vision." NOS says, "I got it, do your thing."

As the gunship came around the ridge, the flares floated down, igniting at low altitude.

Pilot says, "NOS, you got him?" NOS responds, "I'm tracking with optical, the flares blanked out my scope, fire at will."

With the flares igniting so low, the enemy gunner was suspicious and began firing wildly into the sky.

NOS says, "Go ahead dumb shit, keep firing wildly, now we know where you are."

Capt. Wisner rolled in to line up his sights. Despite the bright flare light, he eased his finger onto the red button on his control wheel and gave a loving squeeze.
Once again, the angry bees on the gun deck awoke, spewing red ribbons of death at the enemy gun position.

The gunships orbit took it around to the backside of the ridge. The pilot asked the gunners, "How we doing on ammo?"

Lead gunner says, "The first two are almost out, when they're done, I'll give you the other two, but we'll have to reload."

Pilot says, "I think that's all we'll need to kill this gun." "We don't seem to have any other threats here, so I'll fire out the two guns and then go behind the ridge so you can reload safely." Lead gunner responds, " Roger, Sir."

Capt. Wisner lined up for another pass at the enemy gun. He rolled in again, pouring the remaining rounds of the two miniguns into the gun position.

No response from the enemy indicated possible success.

Pilot says, "We'll do another pass for confirmation."

After one full orbit of the gun's location, Capt. Wisner deemed the gun had been neutralized.

Pilot says, "Copilot, give DASC a call with an update and see where they need us next."

Capt. Wisner asks the crew, "While we wait for DASC's response, let's look for more flashes on the ground."

DASC responded that no more rocket and mortar rounds were impacting the area.

Therefore, they released Shadow 60 from their mission. It was homeward bound for the crew.

Overall, it was a very successful mission.

Shadow 60 returned to base. While their plane was refueled and rearmed, the crew took the opportunity for a meal at the flightline cafeteria.

After a relaxing meal, the crew returned to Squadron Ops to finish out their Alert Duty

Chapter 7
Opening the gates of hell

Smokey 3 contacts Shadow 78, "Shadow 78, could you head over to where my jets are holding? About 10 clicks east of here. They're reporting a 51 Cal down there, causing them grief. I've got my jets holding high and away, that 51 Cal is near the run-in to the camp."

Shadow 78, "Happy to oblige, Smoky 3. We've got our lights on, we'll do some "Gomer Trolling" and get that gun off your boys' backs."

Shadow 78's copilot, Capt. Bill Barnes, said he sees the jets' navigation lights to the gunship's right, in the distance.

Major Mark Johnson, the pilot, asks Bil for specific directions. Bill responds, "Come right 90 degrees for 10 clicks, and get ready to bank left. Charlie will surely see us and open fire."

The pilot calls back to the gunners, "Give me two guns, high rate, and get ready for a firefight.

Alpha gunner Pulaski armed guns number 1 and 3 and selected a high rate of fire.

Bravo gunner Warrick popped the lids off a few ammo cans and positioned them behind minigun stations 1 and 3.

Warrick positioned himself at the troop door to spot for ground fire.

As the gunship neared the location of the 51 Cal, its tracers could be seen probing the night sky towards the jets.

Edging closer to the enemy gun, the gunship's lights caught the attention of the gun crew, who swung their gun around to meet the gunship's path.

In an instant, the enemy unleashed a burst of gunfire at the gunship, which countered with a barrage of 1000 rounds, spewed from the two miniguns.

Silence.

Major Johnson ushered the gunship around the enemy's location for a full 360-degree orbit.

Silence.

Major Johnson told the rear cabin crew to stay alert for additional gunfire. He directed Alpha gunner to keep the current gun settings hot, in case we needed to re-engage. Pulaski acknowledged with a "Roger, Sir."

Halfway through the second orbit, the enemy gun sprang to life and began spraying tracer rounds haphazardly towards the gunship. For a brief moment, the IO reported hearing metallic "thud" sounds, which he thought to be non-lethal hits to the aircraft.

The NOS operator, Capt. John Dickson advised the pilot that he was tracking the resilient enemy gunner. Major Johnson acknowledged he was taking direction from the NOS, as he hauled the big black war machine into another bank.

The moving reticle of his gunsight quickly aligned with the fixed reticle, indicating he was in sync with what the NOS was tracking.
A gentle push of the red button on his control wheel and two high-speed chainsaws sprang to life, hurling thousands of rounds towards the enemy gun position.

Silence once again.

The gunship completed two full orbits, while the NOS continued tracking the target area.

Pulaski took guns #1 and 3 offline for reloading, after arming guns #2 and 4.

Finally, silence. Target neutralized.

"Smokey 3, This is Shadow 78. Smokey 3 here, go ahead, Shadow."

"Smokey 3, your problem has been neutralized. Tell your boys to go get 'em.

We're heading back towards the camp, but we'll stay out of your way."

"Thanks a lot Shadow," said Smokey 3.

Mustang, this is Smokey 3, "I'm ready with the CBU's, how copy?"

Smokey 3, this is Mustang, read you 5 by. I have a change of plans. My West wall and wire have been secured." "Charlies on the east side of my runway, so we want the CBUs about 100 meters east of the east side of the runway, I said the east side of the runway. Run them north to south. We want the Nape along the same path, but 100 meters further east. We can whip their asses if you can do this!"

Spear 3, Spear 4, Arrow 5, Arrow 6, "This is Smokey 3, we are almost ready for your runs. I will mark your target with a rocket and tell you when to execute."

Spear 3 (flight of jets armed with CBUs), "This is Smokey 3, you are cleared hot, from north to south, 100 meters east of the east side of the runway."

"Spear 4 (second flight of CBU jets), you are cleared hot, follow Spear 3's lead with 30 seconds separation. East side of the runway, 100 meters east."

Arrow 5 (flight of Napalm-armed jets), "This is Smokey 3, you are cleared hot for a run following Spear 4, with 2 minutes separation. Your run is north to south on the east side of the runway but put your stuff 100 meters east of where Spears 3 and 4 made their drops."

"Arrow 6, I want you to follow Arrow 5 with a 2-minute separation."

Spear 3 and 4, Arrow 5 and 6, this is Smokey 3. "All you boys be aware that we have a slow-mover gunship operating on the west side of the camp.
We also have a Moonshine flare ship overhead, but it should be high enough to be no sweat. At the end of your runs, veer to the east for safe separation."

Mustang, this Smokey 3, "I have four flights of jets ready to pounce. Do I have clearance?"

"Smokey 3, you have clearance to commence your runs. This will be a fantastic show for our boys."

With the lull in aerial support, the enemy troops have regrouped for another mass attack.

Undaunted by heavy casualties, waves of fighters proceeded to attack the camp, supported by mortar fire and satchel charges. Masses of dead soldiers were still strewn throughout the west wire. But still they came, unrelenting in their determination.

The enemy was unaware of what was in store for them.

This is Smokey 3; "I've fired my marker at the east side of the runway at the north end." "The Command is execute, execute." "Spear 3, Spear 4, start your runs. Arrow 5, Arrow 6 follow Spear flights, but 100 meters east."

As Spear 3 made its run east of the runway, the CBU's spewed hundreds of bomblets from underwing containers.
At ground level, enemy soldiers scrambled for cover, to no avail.

Seemingly endless streams of bomblets rained from the flare-lit sky over the beleaguered camp. Bodies were strewn across the runway mid-stride. Enemy soldiers screamed in agony as they were cut down during their charge towards the Americans' bunkers.

Survivors of the initial strike by the jets hastened to retreat, but were met by the second flight of CBU armed jets.

The sizable enemy force was being whittled down to smaller platoons, intent on making a hasty retreat to the safety of the surrounding jungle.

Those who managed to survive the 100-meter dash to safety were met with the Arrow flight of Napalm-armed jets.

Remaining enemy troops seeking the protection of the jungle suffered the devastation of the firestorm created by the Napalm strikes. Very few survived.

Despite their comrades being decimated on the east side of the runway, enemy troops appeared to be regrouping for a final assault on the camp.

The West Wall had been secured, and the East side of the runway no longer offered a path to the camp.

The sole remaining avenue of attack was the south end of the camp.

Beneath the smoke and haze, faintly illuminated by the flares kicked out by Moonshine, the East and West sides of the camp appeared as if they were the targets of a nuclear strike.

Cratered terrain was flanked by charred vegetation and enemy soldiers. The perimeter of the camp, once cleared for protection, was now a scene of complete devastation.

Four flights of jets, bereft of ordnance and their sortie complete, along with Smokey 3, departed with thanks from Mustang and Ski for a job well done.

Silence was an ominous reprieve from the intensity of battle, save for the droning of the Moonshine flare ship above and Shadow 78 in a holding pattern a few clicks away from the camp.

Shadow 78, this is Mustang. "Are you up?"

Mustang, "This is 78. We are about 5 clicks East of your camp. We've been watching the fireworks show from a safe distance. How may we help?"

"Well, 78, I think Charlie's trying to regroup for a final assault. This must be a battalion of Zombies; the suckers just keep on coming."

"Anyway, I want you to come on over to the South side of the camp since the jets are gone."

"Give me a holler when you get here, I want you to orbit the camp and tell me if you see any activity."
"How copy?"

"Okay, Mustang, 78 copies, we're on our way now."

"Nav to Pilot, how about a heading back to the camp."

"Pilot, this is Nav, come left to 220, that should get us lined up for the camp. Roger Nav, thanks."

As Maj Johnson brought the gunship around, he said "Ah, now I see the camp, thanks Nav."

"Gunners, this is Pilot, you boys cleaned up and ready for another fight?"

Alpha gunner responds "Sure thing sir, we're ready to rock and roll some more. We've got almost 20,000 of ammo left."

Maj Johnsons replies, "Thanks boys, Alpha gunner, give me one-gun hot, low rate, just in case we need to shoot quickly." "You got it sir, said Alpha gunner."

Maj Johnson brought his gunship to the south end of the runway and struck an orbit. He directed the crew to be on the lookout for any activity.

Bravo gunner and the IO took their positions as scanners,

The IO advised the Pilot, "Sir, looks like we have a group of troops assembling about 50 meters from the end of the runway."

Pilot to NOS, "NOS take a peek with the scope and verify what's there."
"Copilot, give Mustang a call, see if he's got any of his people at that location."

Mustang, "This is Shadow 78, looks like we may have some possibles gathering 50 meters off the south end of the runway."

Mustang responds, "Copy that Shadow, hey Ski, we got some activity on the south end of the runway. Are those any of your guys?" "Can you get a Reaction Force out there to confirm?"

Ski says, "Ok Mustang, they're heading over there, will give you a sitrep when they get there."

Shortly after the Reaction Force arrives, the radio erupts with panicked chatter, "Ski, this is Romeo 4, we are engaged with a sizable force, we are outgunned and withdrawing, request assistance ASAP!"

Romeo 4, this is Ski, "Pull your people back minimum 50 meters, we have a gunship overhead just waiting to assist." "Romeo 4, contact Shadow 78 on 48.80, like right now, correct his fire." Romeo 4 responds, "Roger, we're pulling back for front row seats."

Shadow 78 this is Romeo 4, "What's your location?"
Shadow 78 responds, "Look up."
Romeo responds, "Whoa! I got ya babe."

Shadow 78 says, "Romeo 4, I've got a group in my sights, I'll send a short burst, please correct my fire."
Romeo, "Sure thing."

Maj Johnson cuts loose with a short burst.

Romeo 4 responds, "You've got their attention, and they're trying to bug out." "Shoot about 25 meters to the southwest, and you'll pin them down."

Shadow responds, "25 meters southwest, confirmed?" "Here comes a long burst."

Romeo 4 responds, "Good shooting, can you make a ring of fire around that point?" Shadow says, "Sure thing, how's this?"

Maj Johnson calls back to Alpha gunner, "I want to have a continuous stream till I let off the trigger. Can you fix me up?"

Alpha gunner says, "I'll control the switches to make it seamless for you."

"Thank you, Gunner."

Romeo 4, this is Shadow 78, "Here's your ring of fire."

Maj Johnson looked over his left shoulder at his gunsight for reference, confirmed with the NOS he was on the right spot, then squeezed and held his trigger down, painting a circle of death surrounding the enemy soldiers below. It was not really a circle; it was more like a rounded box.

Meanwhile, Alpha gunner worked the gun control switches to achieve non-stop gunfire. As one gun depleted its ammo, he seamlessly switched to another gun. It was a thing of beauty. For the enemy troops, not so much.

Romeo 4 reports to Shadow 78, "They're running around in disarray, like sheep without a sheepdog." "Great job, Shadow."

Shadow, this is Mustang. "Go cease fire and let's see what they're going to do."
"If they decide to attack, you're cleared to take care of business."

"Okay, I'm ceasefire," said Shadow. "I'm pulling off and orbiting your bunkers."

Romeo 4, this is Mustang, "If they decide to surrender, disarm them and take them captive."

After seemingly an eternity, Romeo 4 says, "They are gathering for something." Romeo 4 calls for Shadow 78 to return to the target area.

Romeo 4: "I hear multiple whistle blasts, and the group is dispersing into small teams." "They are running full tilt towards our bunkers, firing their AK-47s as they charge us."

Shadow 78, this is Romeo 4, "Do your thing before they get to us in the bunkers."

Shadow 78 responds, "Roger, we're rolling in now."

Maj Johnson calls back to the gunners, "Give me two, high rate."

Alpha gunner responds, "You got it, sir!"

Two fierce buzzsaws spun up and shredded the attacking force.

Maj Johnson calls back to the gunners, "When these two run out, go to one-gun, low rate." "That'll give you guys time to reload." "Roger, sir, one-gun low rate coming right up."

As soon as the two minis depleted their ammo, Alpha gunner switched over to #2 at low rate. He said to the Pilot, "One-gun, low rate."

Maj Johnson asked the NOS to survey the target area for signs of life.

NOS said, "I'm only picking up bodies, Pilot." "No signs of movement at this time."

Romeo 4, this is Shadow 78, "We're not picking up any signs of life from the enemy troops. We'll go ceasefire if you want to do a sweep."

Romeo 4 says, "Roger that, I've got a team going out there to assess the KIA, I don't think there are enough enemy troops left for you to be concerned."

Shadow 78 responds, "Roger, we'll just cruise around overhead, just in case you need us."

Maj Johnson called back to the gunners, "We're going ceasefire for a while, looks like we may be finished for tonight." "Gunners, give an ammo count when you're done reloading." "If you need to clean up the gun bay, now would be a good time."

"Alpha gunner, leave me one-gun hot, low rate."

"You got it, sir," said Alpha gunner.

Pulaski and Warrick proceeded to reload their respective miniguns. Upon completion, they gathered up the ammo cans of links and brass and stowed them on the floor of the gun bay.

As all four of the miniguns were reloaded and standing at the ready, Warrick secured the ammo boxes to the floor with cargo straps.

Pulaski did a visual check of the gun bay, pronouncing it all secure.

Alpha gunner announced to the Pilot, "All secure back here, sir. All four minis are ready if you need them." "We have 7,500 rounds left, sir."

The IO added, "IO station secure too, sir."

Maj Johnson said, "Good job, boys. I think we can relax for a bit."

NOS reports to the Pilot, "Looks like the Reaction Force has swept the area, and is returning to their camp."

Mustang, this is Shadow 78. "Looks like your people are done with their sweep." "We're going to loiter about 5 clicks to the east until the sun comes up." "We still have 7500 rounds left, if you need them."

Mustang responds, "Roger that, you've done an amazing job here, thanks for sticking with us."

Ski, this is Mustang. "How're your boys doing?"
"Tom, I got two KIA, and a handful of wounded."
"The reaction force just came back, and they're briefing my CC." "My CC has called for a medivac."
"I have a platoon sweeping the camp, making sure we've got everybody accounted for."

Mustang, "This is Moonshine, come up."
"Go ahead Moonshine, I'm up."

Moonshine continues, "I'm starting to see the morning dazzle. You need any more illume?"

Mustang says, "Negative Moonshine, I think we're done with flares, thank you for lighting us up tonight." Moonshine returns with "Our pleasure, call us if you need us, Moonshine out."

Silence returns to the camp, except the distant drone of Shadow 78.

Maj Johnson tells his crew, "I'm going to go back to the camp and make a few orbits before we leave." "Sun's almost up, we don't need to be out here in the daylight." "Scanners keep an eye out for small arms fire; we don't need someone hurt from potshots."

As the black giant makes its way back to the camp, sunlight begins to scatter through the morning mist and the residual smoke engulfing the battle zone.

Hundreds of meters out from the camp, the scene was of absolute devastation.

Singed and charred brush and bodies, some still hanging from the burnt barbed wire strung along the perimeter. As the camp drew near, the eastern side of the runway was littered with dead enemy soldiers.

Maj Johnson brought his gunship into an orbit over the West Wall and wire. Despite the hard bombs' delivery 300 meters away, the western side of the camp suffered major destruction, leaving felled trees, massive craters, bodies, and body parts scattered throughout the tangled concertina wire.

Passing through the south end of the runway, the scene continued with bodies littering the runway's end.

Carnage wrought by two sections of helicopter gunships, two Shadow gunships, and multiple Tac Air strikes.

The camp and its personnel were saved, but reportedly, less than a week later, the camp was overrun by the North Vietnamese Army, remaining in enemy hands until the end of hostilities.

Chapter 8
A Good Landing

Starlight this is King 07, I just heard you talking to Stinger 55, how far is he from my location?

King 07, I have him about 40 clicks from your location, what is your situation?

Starlight, we are conducting a CSAR near Parrot's Beak, we've got an A7 driver down. We also have a problem with small arms and a 23mm that's hampering our search. Any chance you could direct Stinger 55 our way for some Triple A suppression?

Starlight copies, let me contact Stinger 55 to see if they can assist. Starlight out.

Stinger 55, this is Starlight, any chance you can divert 40 klicks to do Triple A suppression for a CSAR?

This is Stinger 55. We can assist. We're not picking up any vehicle traffic tonight. Coordinates please.

Stinger 55, your target area is 40 clicks southwest, contact King 07 for direction. How copy?

Stinger 55 copies all, we're on our way.

Capt Jackson, the pilot, aka "Jack." asks the Nav for a heading. Nav says 200 degrees for 40 clicks.

Jack requests the gunners to go to pre-target for all 6 guns, 4 miniguns and 2 20mm Vulcans.

Alpha gunner later responds, Pre-target complete, sir. You have all six ready for action.

Jack explains to the crew; we're tasked for Triple A suppression for some Jollies and a C-130 on a CSAR mission. Gunners be ready to go guns hot. Scanners keep on your toes; we will be tangling with a 23mm and some small arms.

Jack asks Nav, Let me know when we're about 5 clicks out.

We'll probably start picking up Triple A at that point. Roger, says the Nav.

About 20 mins later, Nav advises Jack that they're 5 clicks out.

Jack announces over the intercom, all right, boys, we should be getting their attention real soon, so look alive. NOS and Sensor, you guys up?

Both responded, we got our eyes on and are watching for the baddies.

King 07, this is Stinger 55, we are 5 clicks from your location. Are you taking fire?

Stinger 55, this is King 07, we're out of the 23's range. We were also picking up some 51 Cal from the same area. King 07, you might want to maintain your position until we finish these guys.

Roger, we'll stay clear, says King 07.

Suddenly, the right scanner breaks in, small caliber fire, four o'clock, no sweat.

Jack alerts everyone, ok crew, looks like we've got a party! Alpha gunner, let's troll a bit, give me one mini, low rate. We're high enough that the mini will tease the little guy.

I'm going to swing around towards the 51 cal and give him a burst. Hopefully, the 23mm will think we're a Shadow and join the party. Gunner, standby to switch to a 20mil.

Gunner here, ready to go sir.

NOS and Sensor, let me know if you pick up where he is.

Jack swings his big bird around to the right, then levels out. Sensor to Pilot, I'm picking up some heat sources about 40 degrees off the nose.

Jack asks his copilot, you have a visual yet,? Copilot responds, not yet. Jack says, okay, I'll swing her around some more, we should pick up something.

NOS and Sensor, any bites yet? Not yet, they answered.

Ok, let's unzip our fly and see what happens. Gunner go guns hot on one mini, low rate, I'll shoot some trees and see who's awake down there.

Jack squeezes his trigger, and a buzz saw awakens on the gun deck. A lazy stream of tracers snakes its way down towards the trees. The gunship is high enough, the impact of the rounds are ineffective. But the point was to make the gunship's presence known to the enemy.

Jack asks his copilot, "Shall we waste a few more rounds on this guy?" Copilot says, "Sure why not?"

Ok NOS, you got a bead on this guy? NOS responds, yup, got him sighted in, let's piss him off a bit. Gunner, go to high rate on that mini.

Roger, you got it, says Alpha gunner.

A furious stream of rounds streak towards the enemy gun position, causing a response from the enemy, who sent a long burst skyward in search of the gunship.

Two mortal enemies, locked in a futile battle. Both out of range of each other.

Jack calls back to the gun deck, Alpha gunner, let's go to the 20, maybe this guy's big brother will join the dance.

Alpha gunner, Roger sir, one mini cold, one 20 hot.

Pilot Jack calls back, Sensor gimme a bead on this guy, I want to agitate that 23.

Sensor to Pilot, I got him, fire when ready!

Named for the Norse god Vulcan, the 20 comes to life with a loud, angry growl, spitting its lethality through cordite smoke and flames.

A few hundred rounds of high-explosive projectiles impacted the gun emplacement, setting off a chain reaction of small explosions, likely from the enemies' ammo cache.

The gunship completed a full orbit, and no response from the enemy confirmed the enemy had been neutralized.

As the gunship rolled wings level, a burst of 23mm rounds streaked across its nose.

The copilot says with excitement, I think we've been noticed!

Jack asks NOS and Sensor to find the 23's location.

NOS quickly responds, I got him Jack, I'm tracking, follow your gunsight.

Jack calls back to the gun bay, Alpha gunner, do I still have that 20 online? Gunner says, "You still got her, she's got plenty of HEI." Jack continues, "Put that mini back online, let's confuse the 23's gunner with an assortment of party favors."

"Okay, boys, we've got us a fight, hang on!"

Jack hauled the old but mighty gunship around like a sports car, NOS said, "Okay, got him in my sights."

Jack calls out to the crew, "Scanners watch for any more small stuff, Sensor, cover our Starboard side."

Depressing his trigger, Jack sends down a fury of rounds towards the 23mm gun, as the enemy gunner attempts to dial in on the gunship. Lethal rounds from the two enemies cross paths inflight. The 20mm rounds dance around the enemy. The 23mm rounds inch ever closer to the gunship.

Suddenly, right scanner calls, that last burst put some holes in the tail fins.

Jack responds quickly, "Roger scanner, gunner, gimme both 20s and another mini on high rate. Let's get this guy!"
"NOS, you still got him? Roger that, fire when ready."

Jack rolled his gunship in a little tighter, lined up the gunsight reticle, and blasted away at the 23, just as the 23 sent a long burst skyward.

The combined lethality of both 20mm Vulcans, caused the 23mm site to explode in a column of flame and smoke. "Got him, resounded Jack!"

Jack, this is copilot, "We've got a problem here." "Speak to me, says Jack."

"We got that 23, but his burst took out a chunk of our starboard wing." Jack tells the Flight Engineer to check out how badly we've been hurt. The Flight Engineer says, "Got it."

A quick review of the gunship's gauges revealed they were losing fuel. It was too soon to establish the rate of loss, but Jack determined they would have to exit the scene and recover at the nearest base.

Nav contacted King 07. "This is Stinger 55, we've neutralized that Triple A for you, it's safe to continue your CSAR." "Be advised, we've taken some damage and we're heading for a base to recover." "Any chance you could spare a Jolly to follow us in case we have to leave our girl in the jungle?"

We also must jettison our flares to lighten the plane. We can launch about two dozen flares. Would that help or hinder you?

King 07 to Stinger 55, "I'll have Jollie 47 follow you, although you're faster." "I can't spare a Sandie, so you're on your own there." "It's ok to toss out your flares, no problem for us."

Roger, King 07, "Just wanted to make sure we had a ride home if we had to leave her here."

"Stinger this is King 07," "Thanks for knocking out the AAA." "Consider Jollie 47 as returning the favor." "Godspeed, and hope you make it home."

IO, this is Pilot, launch all the flares and then jettison the launcher. IO says, Roger, out they go.

Gunners, we need to lose as much weight as we can. Alpha gunner, Roger, Sir, weight reduction commencing.

Alpha and Bravo gunners started tossing ammo, cans of brass, and links out the crew door.

Jack called the crew and asked them if there was anything else they could toss. They responded, Negative, Sir.

Jack asked the Nav, What heading should we fly, and where should we land?

Nav said, If we take a heading of 100 degrees, we should make it to Tan Son Nhut, 50 miles away, if we don't run out of fuel.

Jack asked the Flight Engineer, What do you suggest? The FE said, shut down the jets, lean out the recip engines, and try to do a slow climb. We might be able to level out and coast a little bit along the way. I know she glides as well as a submarine flies, but something is better than nothing.

Jack says, ok, FE, make it happen. Let's try Angels 10 and level out, then pull back on the throttles and see what happens.

At least we have Jollie 47 in trail, in case of a bailout. I hope they have enough room for a party of 10. I failed to make a reservation.

The entire back cabin crew sat tensely in the troop seats. All had donned their parachutes, praying they would not be needed.

The agonizing minutes crawled by as the once-powerful gunship and its crew limped their way towards the safety of Tan Son Nhut.

The gunship successfully inched its way to 10 thousand feet. Once there, the FE deftly adjusted the engine controls to maximize fuel efficiency.

Jack came up on the intercom to bolster the crew's spirits, saying, ok, everybody in the back, I want you to move to the left side of the cabin.

Once there, drop your trousers, bend over, and fart. We need extra thrust to make it.

After a long pause, laughter erupted throughout the aircraft. It was just what everyone needed to cut the tension.

Jack once again announced on the intercom, we may be landing on fumes, but we have a fair chance of making it to Tan Son Nhut.

The gunship was now 20 miles away from the destination. The pilot, copilot, and FE discussed their next steps, deciding that now was the time to begin their ever-so-gentle descent towards the air base at Tan Son Nhut.

Jack, wanting to keep the crew informed, informed them of the plane's status and the arrival plan.

The Navigator contacted the DASC (Direct Air Support Center), advising it of the gunship's plight and emergency status. The DASC, in turn, alerted Tan Son Nhut to activate its emergency response teams.

The copilot contacted Tan Son Nhut tower, advising that the gunship only had enough fuel for a straight-in approach. The tower acknowledged, saying that the runway was clear and crash crews were standing by, adding, You are cleared for runway 07 Right.

The Navigator told the pilot, "We only need to make a slight course correction for a straight-in shot.

At 10 miles out, the pilot cautiously turned the ailing gunship left to a heading of 070 degrees.

Jack once again announces on the intercom, ok boys, we are making our final descent into Tan Son Nhut. Please fasten your seatbelts and return your tray tables to the upright position.

The crew chuckled at Jacks' bit of levity.

He continued, We've only got enough fuel for one shot at the landing. No go around. We can't run the engines up for landing and can't use flaps to slow down. We're coasting in for a carrier landing, without a tailhook. We'll be smacking the pavement hard.

I'll ring the bell once, just before we hit the deck. When you hear it, brace for impact. Don't clench your teeth, I won't pay for dental work.

The gunship lined up for a short final and dropped the landing gear. The FE commented, "Pilot, hydraulic pressure is fluctuating wildly."

Jack responded, "Keep your eye on it, we're almost down."

The pilot and the copilot struggled to control the heavy plane as it rapidly descended towards the runway. About a mile or so out, the left engine began to sputter and cough. Alarm surged in the cockpit.

The copilot counted down the altitude as they neared the end of the runway; "400, 300, 200, 100."

Jack gently pulled back on his control wheel, trying to flare the landing, which would be more like a controlled crash. At 200, he sounded the bell once, alerting the crew to their impending touchdown.

Jack called out to the FE, "That cough on the right engine disturbs me."

The ground came up rapidly, and the gunship smacked the pavement, hard! The Korean War vintage cargo hauler did not take kindly to the abuse, snaking its way down the runway.

To add more excitement to the situation, the right engine coughed once and sputtered to a complete stop. As a result, the plane started to veer to the right. Shit! The FE yelled out, we've lost hydraulic pressure! Jack responded, yikes, I've lost nosewheel steering, and we're veering towards the right shoulder.

Without the right engine I can't steer her with engine power. Copilot, quick help me stand on the brakes and stop this thing!

The copilot stomped and held his brakes, aiding Jack's efforts. The plane began to slow, but still headed towards the right shoulder.

Jack advised the crew, "Stay seated, it looks like we're going to do some four-wheeling in the mud."

Jack, straining at his brakes, called the IO, "IO, too bad we didn't bring that anchor with us!"

The big plane slid to a stop, coming to rest, its right main gear just over the edge of the runway.

In the mud.

Whew! Jack, his copilot, and the FE breathed a unanimous sigh of relief.

The Copilot was the first to speak, "Well, that's a first for the record books." The FE chimed in, "I hope we didn't break her too bad."

Jack asked the FE to do shutdown procedures, and then advised the crew, "Ladies and gentlemen, we've arrived at our destination. Please prepare to deplane. Watch your step as the field is muddy."

Jack and his crew deplaned to a waiting crew bus.

Jack told the driver, "To the O Club, drinks are on me!" The driver said, "I was instructed to take you to OPS for a debriefing." Jack responded, "After we have a drink or two."

And so ended another busy night for the USAF gunship mission.

Any landing you can walk away from is a good landing.

Chapter 9
Another Day at the Office

It was early 1969, and the AC-119 Shadow gunship had begun combat operations in South Vietnam.

One of the key improvements over the AC-47 Spooky gunship was the AC-119's night vision capabilities.

That capability enabled the Shadow gunship to fly night patrols, taking the new gunship to the infamous Ho Chi Minh Trail in search of enemy supply convoys.

Location: Phan Rang AB, RVN, 71st SOS
Time: 1900
Mission: Shadow 61, Armed Reconnaissance
Crew: Crew 16, AC, Maj. Bill Burress

"I'm Capt. Rick Hennessey, the copilot."
"Maj. Bill Burress and Crew 16 launched on time at 1900 hours, call sign Shadow 61."

"Our mission tonight is to patrol the Ho Chi Minh trail in the vicinity of Ban Me Thuot."

"By the time we arrive in the area, it should be good and dark; however, we have a quarter moon. That should be enough light for our NOS to pick up any activity."

"NAV, what's our heading to the search area?" Said the Pilot.

Lt. Bodie, the NAV responded, "Take a heading of 340 for 100 miles." The pilot says, "Roger, turning left to 340." The pilot says to the Copilot, "Rick, take the controls, I'm going down to take a whiz and get some coffee, do you want me to bring you something?" "I responded, I got it, Bill, and no thanks. I'll go down when you come back."

Maj. Burress got his coffee, stretched his legs with a walk down the cargo compartment and back, and then climbed back up to the flight deck.

"My turn," I said once Bill regained control. I clambered down the short ladder from the flight deck to the gun deck. I did my business, got some coffee, and interacted with the crew.

Before I returned to my seat, I looked out through the NOS station, the former crew entrance, on the left side of the aircraft.

There, beneath us, were hundreds of craters—reminders of previous Arclight strikes (B-52 carpet bombing missions). In the darkness, under the quarter moon, the craters filled with water reflected the moonlight, sparkling and twinkling as we passed over them.

If you looked closely, you could sometimes catch a reflection of the moon in the water.

There was an eerie beauty that belied the absolute devastation wrought by the explosive impacts of a thousand 500 and 750-pound bombs dropped from the B-52s.

A swath one mile wide and five miles long had been carved out of the jungle.

I climbed into my seat, put on my headset, and listened to the NAV talking to Pyramid Control (Air traffic control radar station for our target sector).

"Shadow 61, this is Pyramid Control. I have you 20 miles out from my location. Will you be staying on your current heading?"

Shadow 61 responds, "That's affirmative Pyramid, we'll be patrolling along the border within the buffer zone."

Pyramid acknowledged saying, "It's been pretty quiet in the sector, hope you're not going to stir up the hornets." Shadow 61 responds, "We're just going to play Highway Patrol for a while."

Pyramid says, "Okay then, give us a call if you need anything, we've got our eyes on you."

Maj. Burress announced on the intercom, "Boys, let's go to pre-target, just in case we need to shoot at something." "Gunner, go guns hot on one gun, low rate, you never know what we might find."

Alpha gunner said, "You got one gun hot, low rate, Sir."

Maj. Burress advised the NAV, "I'm going to fly a route parallel to the border, just inside the buffer."

He added, "NOS, are you up?" NOS says, "Yup, I'm doing a wide scan, just to see if we pick up any lights or hot spots." "I got nothing yet. Maybe Charlie hasn't stopped for dinner yet."

As time passed, I commented to Bill, "Seems like this might be an uneventful night on the Trail."

The NOS broke the silence, "Pilot, I think I have some dim lights under the jungle canopy. I'll hit my Track switch, so you know where to orbit."

Maj. Burress says, "I've got it NOS, let's take a closer look." NOS says, "Roger."

Maj. Burress calls to the back, "OK, boys, look alive, we may have found something of interest down below." He continues to the NOS, "What have you got?"

NOS says, "I'm not sure. I see what looks like a camp, but I don't see any vehicles parked nearby."

"I do see some large, indistinct figures gathered under the trees. I'm not sure what they are."

I contacted the ABCC to confirm no friendlies were in the area. They gave us clearance to fire.

I said to the pilot, "Bill, no friendlies, and we're cleared to fire." Bill responded, "Roger that, let's ruin someone's dinner plans." "Gunners, I'm going to send a short burst down range." The gunners said, "Go for it, we're ready."

Maj. Burress says to the NOS, "I'll fire a short burst when we get parallel to the Trail, just in case someone down there wants to shoot back."

NOS says, "I'm still tracking, fire at will."

As Maj. Burress brought the gunship around, he pushed his trigger, waking up the sleeping minigun, launching a few hundred rounds down to the dinner party.

NOS said, with excitement, "We got some pops and flashes when those rounds hit." Maj. Burress said, "Hmm, maybe we should see what else we can light up." "Ok, here comes a long burst, I'm going to wag the wings for greater dispersion."

Towards the end of this burst, something big exploded! The NOS said, "Holy shit. That was an exploding elephant, Bill." Maj. Burress responded, "A what?" NOS said,

"Yeah, an exploding elephant." "Those indistinct objects are a small herd of elephants."

Bill remarked, "Geez, I hate to kill the suckers, but Charly's apparently using them to haul ammo and explosives."

"Bill and I talked it over and concluded that, as distasteful as it was, we had an obligation to destroy the supplies that would later be used to kill our boys and allies." "It was a difficult decision to make, but we agreed."

Bill asked me to call the ABCC for confirmation.

I described what we had found as a target. The ranking staff member aboard the ABCC gave us the go-ahead to eliminate the herd.

Maj. Burress announced on the intercom our situation, advising all of what we are about to do.

Receiving no dissenting opinions, he called back, "Gunners, give me two guns, high rate. We must make this as quick and painless as we can."

Maj. Burress asked the NOS, "Is the herd grouped or are they strung out?" NOS said, "They are huddled around the one we killed."

"OK, let's do this and get out of here." Said Maj. Burress. "This is going to be hard to write up in my mission report." NAV says, "We have the ABCC's directions on tape, in case there's an inquiry."

Maj. Burress rolled the gunship into a firing orbit, squeezed his trigger, and sent 3,000 rounds of death down into the elephant herd. The stream of fire caused multiple explosions, some with such concussive force that the aircraft was rocked back and forth.

Maj. Burress performed a few more orbits, confirming success. Afterwards, he announced to the crew that the target had been neutralized.

Bill and I discussed what to do next. We had plenty of fuel and ammo left. We decided to contact ABCC for clearance to patrol southwest near the trail.

I contacted the ABCC, gaining clearance to extend our patrol to the southwest.

It was a quiet flight until the tranquility was abruptly shattered by one of the scanners shouting, "Triple A three o'clock, no sweat!"

I commented to Bill, "Who the hell is shooting at us?" I asked on the intercom, "Who's got eyes on that gun?" Bravo gunner said, "Bravo gunner here, it looked bigger than a 51 Cal, Sir." "It looked like it was coming from across the border." I thanked the gunner and asked Bill whether we should engage or continue our patrol.

He responded, "At this point, we wouldn't derive any benefit by engaging." "I wouldn't want to take her home all banged up."

We agreed to continue patrolling.

NAV broke the silence, saying, "We need to come left to 250 degrees to stay on our side of the border." Bill said, "Roger NAV, I'm turning to 250 degrees."

I said to Bill, "Looks pretty darn quiet out here tonight. What do you think about making a slow cruise back to Poppa Romeo (Phan Rang)?"

Bill agreed, saying, "NAV, how about a heading back home?" NAV responded, "A 140 could get us home pretty quickly." Bill asked me. "Can you take the controls while I make a pitstop?"

"Sure thing."

About 30 clicks along our current heading, the radio awoke with a plaintive whisper, "This is Greasy Spoon 4 to aircraft overhead." "We are surrounded and overwhelmed by Charlies." "We need assistance!" "Please wag your wings or toggle your lights if you can hear us."

Bill told the FE to toggle our nav lights, which he did.

"Greasy Spoon 4, this is Shadow 61, give us a sitrep, please," I asked the Nav to call ABCC and advise them of the situation and the players. "We'll need to be cleared to assist."

"Shadow 61, this is Greasy Spoon 4, thank god!" "We wanted you to call for help for us." "Are you able to help us out, brother?"

I said, "Sure thing, Spoon 4, we are a gunship." "We are waiting for clearance from our higher-ups." "While we are waiting, tell us what's going on."

Shadow 61, "We are pinned down against a large rock outcropping." "We are a LRRP (Long Range Recon Patrol), heading back to our camp."

"We were doing Trail recon and got spotted by an NVA force." "We managed to evade the main force and hide in these boulders." "We're trapped here among the boulders, with Charlies all around us."

"They haven't found us yet, but they're getting closer." "I have a whiskey here that was snakebit while hiding in the rocks." "We have him quieted with morph; fortunately, it wasn't venomous."

"We need to get out of here for an extraction and medivac." "Can you help us out?"

I said to Spoon 4, "Once we get clearance, we should be able to fix you up." "We're packing 25,000 rounds of 7.62 and flares."

Spoon 4 responds, "Yeah, that should even things up a bit."

I also added, "While waiting, we'll orbit overhead with our night scope and watch the Charlies." "Stay on this channel, and we'll take care of you."

Spoon 4 said, "Sure thing."

In the time it took for three full orbits, ABCC cleared us for contact.

I called Spoon 4 and said, "We've got clearance to engage the enemy troops." "Our control also notified Ban Me Thuot of your location and need for an ambulance and taxi service." "They are on their way for you."

I continued, "Spoon 4, are all your people up in the rocks?" "We don't want to smack any of your guys."

"Shadow 61, this is Spoon 4, I got my boys down, is it showtime?"

I said, "Spoon 4, this is Shadow 61, we'll lay down a sample burst, correct our fire if you need to."

Bill called the gunners for "One gun, low rate."

"Pilot, gunner, you got one low, sir."

Bill also said, "Gunners, prepare for a little bit of work, we've got some friendlies pinned down, we're going to fix that." The gunners, Rogers and Rickert, said, "You got it, Sir, ready when you are."

"NOS, you tracking?" NOS said, "I'm tracking."

Bill wheeled her over into a left bank and sent a storm of red tracers towards the enemy troops.

I called down to Spoon 4, "How's that look?"

Spoon 4 replied, "Looks pretty good, you got a bunch of them, but they're trying to hide."

I said to Spoon 4, "Would it help you if I punched out a flare so you could see them?" Spoon 4 said, "Give it a try." I told the IO, "IO, launch a flare, now."

The IO said, "Flare away."

A minute later, the flare ignited, casting a broad, bright yellow light across the area.

I said, "How's that, Spoon 4?" He said, "That's helpful, we can pick them off when we see them."

I asked the NOS, "Can you see the little buggers better?" The NOS said, "Yup, if you can spray in a broad arc, we should be able to turn this around for Spoon 4."

Bill says, "Okay, gunner, give me two, low rate." Rogers said, "You're on!"

Bill started the two-gun burst as he entered his turn. He held down the trigger to describe an arc down below, slightly wagging his wings to disperse the rounds."

Spoon 4 said, "That's excellent, you've killed most of them, and the survivors are running scared." "I think you've saved us. Thank you, Shadow."

I responded to Spoon 4, "You're welcome, we'll stick around until your rides get here." He said, "Good deal." "They're sneaky little bastards; they'll probably hide and take pot shots at the choppers."

I tried to assure Spoon 4, "If they do, we'll make sure those are the last potshots they'll ever take."

"A face full of 7.62mm rounds will change their life." Spoon 4 said, "I hear that!"

Spoon 4 added, "I hear the choppers, I'm going to pop smoke for them."

I asked him, "Would flare light help?" He said, "It might highlight the choppers for Charley, so I'd skip the flares."

The Medivac chopper swooped in and picked up the injured soldier and a few others.

The Medivac took off, and another chopper took its place, extracting part of the LERP team. Another was inbound when all hell broke loose!

Charley started firing at the choppers, and a 51 Cal began shooting at us! Fortunately, we were in orbit and brought our guns to bear against the small arms firing at the choppers. We were able to minimize the small arms threat to the departing choppers, but the 51 Cal was becoming a problem. A problem that we needed to deal with, as the choppers were not yet out of the 51 Cal's range.

Bill called up the gunners, asking for all four guns, high rate, saying, "Let's end this once and for all!"

Bill said, "NOS, I'm coming around that gun's location, let me know when he's firing towards the choppers and distracted." "I'm giving him a ticket for a dirt nap." NOS says, "I'm on it."

The gunship came around almost behind the 51 Cal gun, as it was firing some last futile shots at the choppers fading from view.

The NOS yelled, "Now!" Bill pressed his trigger, and instantly, 6,000 angry rounds sped towards the enemy gunner.

The enemy gunner spotted the ensuing firestorm, spun around, and fired his last earthly rounds towards the gunship.

In moments, the battle was over.

The LRRP had been rescued, with no further losses.

It was a good night's work for Crew 16.

After signing off from the ABCC, it was time to RTB.

Maj. Burress and Crew 16 were on their way home.

En route to Phan Rang, Art, the FE, noticed that oil pressure seemed to be dropping on the number 1 engine. Bill, Rick, and Art discussed the dropping oil pressure, deciding to monitor it during the flight home.

During their final approach to Phan Rang, they lowered the landing gear in preparation for landing.

The gear doors opened, and the main gear lowered with a loud "thunk."

Bill called back to the IO, "Tito, check the port landing gear, report what you see." "We've been losing oil pressure on number one all the way home."

Tito said, "I'm taking a look right now." "Looks like one of the hoses in the gear bay got nicked." "I see oil streaming from the hose, and the inside of the gear doors is coated with oil."

Bill said, "Ok, thanks, Tito, keep watching it until we're almost down." "I'll tell you when to get in your seat for landing." "Roger, Sir," Tito said.

The crew was all set for touchdown as they neared the end of the runway. Bill said, "Tito, go ahead and take your seat." "Ok, Sir." "Holy Shit!" yelled Tito into the intercom. "Sir, we have a fire in the port landing gear bay." Bill told Tito, "Take your seat and strap in, we'll just ride her down, we can't risk hitting the fire bottle and killing that engine at this point." "As long as number one is making power and we can control it, it'll be okay."

I called the tower and told them to launch the crash trucks; we had a fire on the port side.

As we touched down, the crash trucks were on the taxiway, rushing towards us.

Bill said he could see the bright glow of the burning engine compartment reflected off the runway.

As the big gunship came to a halt, Bill applied power to the engines and slowly rolled onto an adjacent taxiway, clearing the runway for other aircraft.

The crash crew put out the fire as Bill shut down the number one engine.

The crew gathered their personal gear and calmly waited for the crew bus. Art and the crew conducted a visual inspection of the landing gear bay, revealing that a 51-caliber round had nicked an oil hose.

One of the fuel lines appeared to have had heat damage from the oil fire. It was pure luck that the fuel line hadn't split, causing a major fuel fire.

The fire was hot enough to burn the skin off the landing gear door.

Soon, an aircraft tug would arrive to tow the injured gunship back to its parking spot.

Just another day at the office.

Chapter 10
Air Commando Spirit

In 1968, Air Commando Squadrons were renamed "Special Operations Squadrons."

Despite the renaming, the Air Commando Spirit remained within the new squadrons.

Adaptability and innovation were traditions established by the original Air Commandos in World War II. The Special Operations Squadrons of the Vietnam War continued these traditions.

During the Vietnam War, in the early 70's, the Shadow gunships were turned over to the VNAF.

The USAF Shadows' mission was inherited by the Stinger Gunship, initially deployed for truck hunting on the Ho Chi Minh Trail.

During truck-hunting missions, the Stingers encountered increasingly dangerous AAA guns, ranging from .51Cal to 57mm radar-controlled AAA.

The Stingers hunted trucks in tandem with AC-130 Spectre Gunships, with Spectres flying into even more deadly regions.

In 1972, North Vietnam introduced the Soviet-supplied Strella.

The SA-7 Strella was an infrared-guided, shoulder-fired missile. In current parlance, it would be considered a MANPAD, or "man-portable air-defense missile."

It proved highly effective against the AC-130 Spectre Gunship, resulting in several losses.

As the Strella threat migrated into South Vietnam, it became a threat to tactical jets.

Following the tradition of innovation, Stingers developed a method to combat the Strella missile.

When a Strella launch was detected by one of the scanners aboard the Stinger, he would call out the location and "break left or break right." At that time, the IO would launch a flare to decoy the missile.

The procedure proved effective, enabling the Stingers to patrol as airborne air defense assets, a unique utilization of the Stinger Gunship, and just one example of the Air Commando Spirit, which lives on today in current Air Commandos.

About the Author

Jim Mattison flew as an Aerial Gunner aboard the AC-119G Shadow gunship.

He was awarded the Distinguished Flying Cross and eight Air Medals, accumulating 750 combat hours, flying 150 missions with the 71st and 17th Special Operations Squadrons.

He is retired and has published 10 children's books and 3 non-fiction titles, all of which are available on Amazon.com

From Jim: "I hope you have enjoyed this novelette. The stories are fictionalized accounts, except the Battle of Duc Phuong and the Shootdown of Jollie 71, which were transcribed from actual mission audio files."

Please consider leaving me a review on Amazon.com

www.ingramcontent.com/pod-product-compliance
Lightning Source LLC
Chambersburg PA
CBHW021922170626
46807CB00007B/2939